NOW YOU CAN READ....

The Elves and the Shoemaker

STORY ADAPTED BY LUCY KINCAID

ILLUSTRATED BY ERIC KINCAID

© 1983 The Rourke Corporation, Inc.

Published by The Rourke Corporation, Inc., P.O. Box 711, Windermere, Florida 32786. Copyright © 1983 by The Rourke Corporation, Inc. All copyrights reserved. No part of this book may be reproduced in any form without written permission from the publisher. Printed in the United States of America.

Library of Congress Cataloging in Publication Data

Kincaid, Lucy.
  The Elves and the shoemaker.

  (Now you can read)
  Reprint. Originally published: Cambridge [Cambridgeshire]: Brimax Books, © 1981.
  Summary: A poor shoemaker becomes successful with the help of two elves who finish his shoes during the night.
  [1. Fairy tales. 2. Folklore—Germany] I. Embleton, Gillian, ill. II. Elves and the shoemaker. III. Title. IV. Series: Kincaid, Lucy. Now you can read.
PZ8.K53El 1983   398.2'1'0943   [E]   82-21600
ISBN 0-86592-179-2

THE ROURKE CORPORATION, INC.
Windermere, Florida 32786

NOW YOU CAN READ....

The Elves and
the Shoemaker

Once there was a shoemaker. He sat at his bench making shoes all day long. He worked very hard but nobody would pay him a fair price for the shoes he made. He and his wife were very poor.

One day, the
shoemaker showed
his wife a piece
of leather.
"This is the last
piece of leather
I have," he said.
"When it is gone
I will be unable
to make any more
shoes. We will
get very hungry.
We may even starve."
"No wonder you look so sad," said
his wife. She was sad herself.

The shoemaker cut out the pieces
for the last pair of shoes. He
put them on the bench.
"It is late," he said. "Let us
go to bed. I will sew the pieces
together in the morning."

"Wife! Wife!" he called loudly next morning. "Come quickly!"

"What is it?" cried his wife. She ran into the workshop. There on the bench was a beautiful pair of finished shoes.

"Did you get up in the night and make them?" she asked.

The shoemaker shook his head.

"Then how did they get there?" she asked.

"I do not know," said the shoemaker.

"Whoever made the shoes meant us to have them" said the shoemaker. "They would not have left them behind if they did not."

He took the shoes to the market. He sold them for a very good price. He and his wife would not starve that day, or the next.

The shoemaker
bought some food.
Plus, he had enough
money left to buy
leather for TWO
more pair of
shoes.
He cut the pieces
for the new shoes.
Then, he laid them
on the bench. "I will
sew them tomorrow,"
he said.

"Wife! Wife! Come quickly!" called the shoemaker next morning. "It has happened again!"

"I do not believe it!" said the shoemaker's wife. There, on the bench, were two pair of finished shoes.

"Look how well they are made," said the shoemaker. "There is not a stitch out of place."

"Fine shoes for sale!" he shouted. when he got to the market place. "Fine shoes for sale!"

He sold both pair in the first five minutes he was there. He was paid a very good price for them too. That day he bought enough leather to make four more pair of shoes.

So it went. Every night the shoemaker left pieces of leather on the bench. Every morning they had been sewn into shoes. Every day he bought more leather.

One day, the shoemaker's wife said, "I wish we knew who is making the shoes for us. We owe everything to them. I would like to say thank you."

"I know how we can find out," said the shoemaker.

That night he put the pieces of leather on the bench as before. He put out the light, as before. Instead of going to bed the shoemaker and his wife hid in the darkest corner of the room. There they waited. At midnight two little elves stepped in through the open window.

They sat cross-legged on the bench
and began to sew. They did not
waste a minute. When they had put
the last stitch into the last shoe
they slipped away as quietly as
they had come.

The shoemaker and his wife hurried to the window.

"We must find a way of thanking them," said the shoemaker.

"The poor little things," said his wife. "Did you notice how ragged their clothes were? Did you see that they had no shoes?"

"I will make them shoes," said the shoemaker.

"I will make them each a set of clothes," said his wife.

The shoemaker took the finest,
softest piece of leather he had.
He made two pair of tiny shoes.
He had never made anything so
small before.

The shoemaker's wife took the finest cloth she could find. She made two sets of tiny clothes. She knitted two pairs of tiny socks. She made two tiny hats. She had never made anything quite so small before.

By Christmas Eve everything was ready. That night the shoemaker put all the shoe leather underneath the bench. On top of the bench he put the two pairs of tiny shoes. His wife laid the two sets of tiny clothes beside them. Then they hid and waited for the elves to come.

When the elves saw what was on the bench they cried out in delight. "These must be for us!" they said. They took off their rags and dressed themselves in their new clothes. They put on their new shoes. They put on their new hats. All the time they smiled and smiled.

The two happy little elves danced
all along the bench.
"Now we are no longer poor,
Shoemaking we will do no more,"
they sang.
Then they skipped out through the
window and were gone.

The shoemaker and his wife never saw the elves again. But, their luck had changed. The shoes the shoemaker made sold as well as the shoes the elves had made. They were never poor again and lived happily ever after.

All these appear in the pages of
the story. Can you find them?

shoemaker

shoemaker's wife

shoes

bench

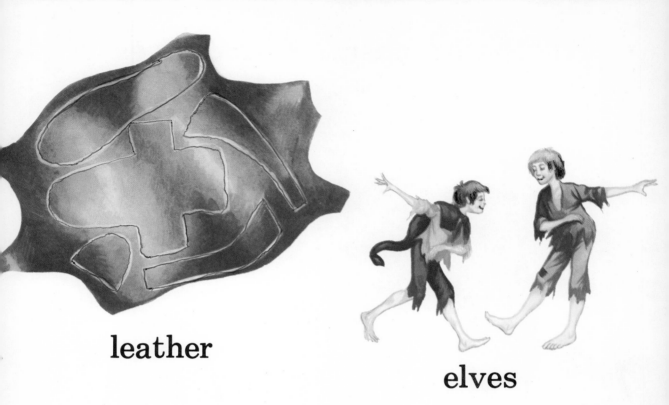

leather

elves

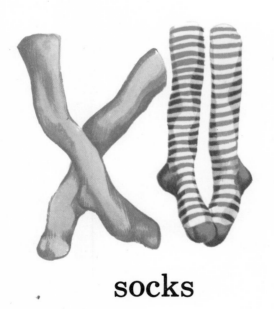

socks

hats

Use the pictures to tell the story in your own words. Then, draw your own pictures.

DATE DUE			
2-B FEB 5	T. 2D	P 5c JAN 30	APR 04
3-AJ MAR 3 5	FEB 8		NOV 8
FEB 5B	*	$130	NOV 21
O 5B	Kulle		NOV 21
FEB 19	MAR 17	F 54	
O-IA JUN	NOV 11	DEC 17	
S/C FEB 15		FEB 9	
		MAR 22	

$9.25   #4068

398.2
K   Kincaid, Lucy.

          The Elves and the
          shoemaker.

621626   10328A